Arthur and the Bad-Luck Brain

Arthur and the Bad-Luck Brain

Text by Stephen Krensky

Based on a teleplay by Gerard Lewis

LITTLE, BROWN AND COMPANY

New York ☙ An AOL Time Warner Company

First Edition

The characters and events portrayed in this book are fictitious.
Any similarity to real persons, living or dead, is coincidental and
not intended by the author.

Arthur® is a registered trademark of Marc Brown.

Text has been reviewed and assigned a reading level by Laurel S. Ernst,
M.A., Teachers College, Columbia University, New York, New York;
reading specialist, Chappaqua, New York.

Library of Congress Cataloging-in-Publication Data

Krensky, Stephen.
Arthur and the Bad-Luck Brain / text by Stephen Krensky ; based on a
teleplay by Gerard Lewis.—1st ed.
p.   cm. — (A Marc Brown Arthur chapter book ; 30)
Summary: The Brain does not believe in superstition, but when he tries
to prove that superstitions are nonsense he starts finding bad luck
everywhere he turns.
ISBN 0-316-12650-0—ISBN 0-316-12377-3 (pbk)
[1. Superstition—Fiction.   2. Aardvark—Fiction.   3. Animals—Fiction.]
I. Title
PZ7.K883Aj 2003
[Fic]—dc21   2003047637

10 9 8 7 6 5 4 3 2 1

WOR (hc)

COM-MO (pb)

Printed in the United States of America

To Robert Freedman

Chapter 1

• • • • • • • • • •

It was a beautiful day for a softball game. The sun was shining. The sky was blue. Unfortunately, the team from Lakewood Elementary School was paying little attention to the weather. Arthur, Buster, Binky, Francine, Muffy, and the Brain were sitting together on the bench — and none of them were smiling.

"Take me out of the ballgame!" Binky was singing to anyone who would listen.

"Excuse me, Binky," said the Brain. "I think you mean, 'Take me out *to* the ballgame.' That's the way the song goes."

Binky shook his head. "No, I mean just

what I said. I want out of this ballgame. We stink!"

The Brain wasn't about to argue with him. Their third-grade team was going down in flames. They were losing badly to Mighty Mountain, one of their biggest rivals. The score was 10–0.

"There's not much time left," said Arthur.

"No kidding," said Francine. "It's the bottom of the ninth with one out."

"There's always time for a miracle," Buster insisted. "Come on, George!" he shouted.

George was at the plate with a full count on him — three balls and two strikes.

In came the pitch — and George gave it his best swing.

And missed.

"Steeerike three!" called out the umpire.

The Brain stood up and put chalk on his hands.

"Now there are two outs!" Francine reminded him. "You're the only one who can help us now."

The Brain straightened up. "You mean help us win?"

"No," said Muffy. "Just help us avoid complete humiliation."

Buster shoved a bat into the Brain's hands. "Use this one," he said. "It's new. Got a lot of hits left in it."

"I don't believe bats are actually made with a specific number of hits," said the Brain. "Even modern science has its limitations."

"Yeah, yeah," said Buster. "Meanwhile, don't forget to spit on the handle."

The Brain frowned. "Why would I do that? It's not hygienic. In fact, it's almost disgusting."

The Brain walked to the plate and stood ready.

The first pitch blew by him.

"Steeerike one!" called the umpire.

"JUST DO IT!" shouted Buster. "IT'S LUCKY!"

"Spitting isn't lucky," the Brain insisted. "It's only a good way to spread germs."

The second ball whizzed by him as well.

"Steeerike two!" said the umpire.

"Come on, Brain."

"You can do it!"

"We really need a hit!"

The Brain called for time and stepped out of the batter's box. He looked back at the bench. "Don't worry. It's all a question of knowing the ratio of ball speed to its trajectory. After compensating for the air resistance, of course."

On the next pitch, he swung hard and sent the ball soaring. Up, up, up it went.

"Go, Brain, go!"

"Turn on the jets!"

The Brain started running around the bases. He passed first and rounded toward second.

The ball was coming down now. Down, down, down. It landed with a thud in the left fielder's mitt.

"Three outs!" called the umpire. "This game's over. Mighty Mountain wins, ten to zero."

Chapter 2

· · · · · · · · · · ·

"It could have happened to anyone," said the Brain, walking home with Buster, Arthur, Francine, and Muffy. "It had nothing to do with me refusing to expectorate."

"Huh?" said Buster.

"Spit," said the Brain. "Not spitting on the bat wasn't a factor."

"How can you be so sure?" said Arthur. "It's a tradition — like smashing a champagne bottle against the side of a new ship. All the pros do it."

"It's not all the Brain's fault," said Buster. "I should have worn my lucky hat."

Francine sighed. "And I should have worn my lucky socks."

The Brain shook his head. "You guys should hear what you sound like. We didn't lose because of bad luck. We lost because they were better than we were today."

"Yeah," said Muffy. "And luckier, too."

The Brain laughed. "You're not serious, are you? I mean, people have had superstitious beliefs since the dawn of civilization. But no one has ever proven them to be true."

"Yeah, yeah," said Buster. "That's what those crazy scientists want you to think. Just because they can't prove something with their formulas and Bunsen burners, they say it isn't true."

"On behalf of scientists everywhere, I must . . ." the Brain began.

"Don't move!" cried Buster.

"Huh? Why not?"

"Look!"

A black cat padded across the sidewalk in front of them and stopped to rub its back against a fire hydrant.

"We have to go the other way," said Buster. "A black cat has crossed our path."

"Yup," said Francine. "We'll have to walk around."

"*Way* around," said Arthur.

Muffy sighed. "I wish I'd called for the limo."

The Brain frowned. "None of you have been listening to a word I've said."

"I listened," said Buster. "You said that no one's ever proven a superstition true. But that doesn't mean they aren't. Look."

He pointed across the street where Mr. Ratburn was walking along the sidewalk. Ahead of him was a tall ladder with an open can of paint perched at the top.

"I'll bet you even Mr. Ratburn doesn't walk under that ladder."

They all watched. Sure enough, Mr. Ratburn came up to the ladder, glanced up, and walked quickly around it.

"See?" said Buster. "He knows it's bad luck to walk under a ladder."

The Brain snorted. "It's also common sense. Why walk under a ladder *and* an open can of paint? It might fall on you."

"Which would be unlucky," said Buster. "Exactly my point."

"That's a terrible argument!" the Brain insisted.

"Call it what you want — it's still the truth."

Buster turned to go — and almost stepped on a crack in the sidewalk.

"Whoa! That was a close one. Step on a crack, break your mother's back."

He continued down the block, awkwardly avoiding the cracks in his way.

"IT'LL BE DARK BEFORE YOU GET HOME!" the Brain shouted after him.

"It'll be worth it," Arthur explained.

"Where his mother's health is concerned," Francine added, "why take chances?"

The Brain rolled his eyes. This superstition thing had to be stopped, and he was the one to do just that.

Chapter 3

Outside the Brain's house, Muffy, Arthur, Binky, Buster, and Francine all sat on folding chairs. The Brain stood quietly before them, wearing a lab coat and holding a pointer. Next to him were some props he had collected. There was an open stepladder, a small sign pointing to a crack in the sidewalk, and a mirror in a cardboard box. Off to one side was a poster stand holding a big chart.

"Thank you," said the Brain, "for agreeing to come to my experiment."

"Are you going to blow something up?"

asked Binky. "I love it when you blow things up."

"Sorry, Binky. Nothing so dramatic today. But it's still important for you to be here. I need witnesses."

"Is this like a trial?" asked Francine. "I want to be the judge."

"No, no," said the Brain. "It's not a trial. Just an exhibition." He paused. "I'd like to draw your attention to Exhibit A — the open ladder."

"It still sounds like a trial to me," Francine muttered. "BRAIN, WHAT ARE YOU DOING?!"

At that moment the Brain was walking under the ladder.

"Are you crazy?" Arthur said.

"That's bad luck!" said Buster.

The Brain ignored them, and walked under the ladder several more times just to make his point. "Remember," he said,

"you're all witnesses. Now for Exhibit B —
the crack."

The Brain broke into a tap dance, his feet
landing squarely on the sidewalk crack
again and again.

"Hey, what about your mother?" asked
Buster. "You're taking her life in your
hands, er, feet."

"Nonsense," said the Brain. "Poppycock,
I might add."

He moved over to the window. "And
finally, Exhibit C. You may want to stand
back a bit."

He picked up the mirror — and dropped
it in the box.

The mirror broke into several pieces.

Everyone gasped.

"Now you've done it," said Arthur.
"That's seven years of bad luck."

The Brain walked over to his chart.
"Nonsense. There is no such thing. And
I'm going to prove it. Over the next few

days I will keep track of any bad things that happen to me. If there is no dramatic increase from the usual number, I will have established the evidence that superstitions are false."

He pointed to his friends with a sweeping gesture. "And *you* will all be witnesses."

Francine bit her lip. "Aren't you even a little bit scared?" she asked.

The Brain folded his arms. "Science does not scare easily."

At that moment, a clap of thunder rumbled overhead, and it started to rain.

"I'm getting out of here."

"Me, too!"

"I don't want to catch his bad luck."

"He's cursed!"

Everyone except the Brain ran away.

"Oh, come on," said the Brain. "I knew it was going to rain. See? I even brought an umbrella."

The Brain opened the umbrella. It kept him dry for a moment — before a gust of wind blew it out of his hands.

And then the Brain got soaked.

Chapter 4

• • • • • • • • • • •

That night at dinner, the Brain was telling his parents about his day.

"And you wouldn't believe it," he said, "but all my friends really believe in this superstitious stuff."

"Some traditions have a long history," said his father.

"And old habits are hard to break," added his mother.

"I know, I know," said the Brain. "Still . . . you'd think they'd demand some proof, some shred of evidence. The whole thing is based on coincidence and fear."

He paused to cut his pork chop, but his knife slipped and fell to the floor.

"Oops," said his mother. "You dropped a knife. You know what that means? We're going to get a male visitor."

The Brain frowned. "Mom, you don't really believe that, do you? Haven't you been listening to what I was saying? All that stuff was cooked up by a bunch of —"

The doorbell rang.

"Who can that be at this hour?" asked the Brain's father.

A little surprised, the Brain went to get the door. Even if someone had come to visit, that didn't mean it was a male visitor. And even if it was, well, the odds of that were fifty-fifty in any case.

He opened the door — and sighed. Binky was standing there.

"Hi, Brain."

"Hi, Binky."

"Brain, I was wondering . . . I bet you don't know what ninety-six divided by twelve is."

"Sure I do. It's eight."

"Thanks," said Binky. He pulled out a piece of paper and wrote down the number.

"How about eight times eight?" he asked.

"Sixty-four."

"Ah." Binky wrote that number on the paper, too. He started to ask another question, but the Brain spoke first.

"Do you want to come in, Binky? We're just finishing dinner. Once we're done, you and I can work on our homework together. Why don't you head up to my room, and I'll be right there."

"Oh, well," said Binky, "if you insist."

When the Brain joined Binky a few minutes later, he found him staring at the bookcase.

"You've got a lot of books here," said Binky.

"That's true," the Brain admitted.

"And they have small print. A lot of words are crammed in there."

The Brain smiled. "Very true. So . . . let's get to work." He looked around for his backpack.

"Binky, you didn't move anything in here, did you?"

"Um, just that raptor model. I thought it was staring at me. So I turned it toward the wall."

"That's okay. But what about my backpack? I always put it right there on my chair."

"Haven't seen it," said Binky.

The Brain sighed. "I must have left it at school."

"Bad luck," said Binky, throwing himself on the bed. "But it's not a total loss. At least we can do our math." He held up his sheet of paper. "I've got questions, and you've got answers."

"I guess," said the Brain. He still didn't believe in luck — good or bad — but he wasn't quite as sure as he had been before.

Chapter 5

· · · · · · · · · · ·

The Brain was walking alone deep inside a dark forest. He didn't like being alone, but he didn't remember having a choice in the matter.

All kinds of noises could be heard in the gloomy underbrush. There were screeches and grunts and chatterings, none of which sounded very friendly.

"I'm lost," he said to himself. "But it's not because I'm unlucky. It's just because I don't know where I am. If I can just find a clearing, I'll take my bearings from the sun. Science can beat luck any day."

At that moment he burst into just the kind of clearing he was hoping for.

"Aha!" he shouted. "My luck is changing." Or it would be, *he thought quickly,* if there were such a thing.

He looked up at the sun — just before it disappeared behind a bank of clouds.

Then it started to rain. Lightning flashed, followed by a roar of thunder.

"Perfectly natural," thought the Brain. "We see the lightning before we hear the thunder simply because light travels faster than sound."

What wasn't so natural, though, was seeing that the thunder had disturbed a herd of wild four-leaf clovers. They started to run in panic, bearing down on the defenseless Brain.

"Oh, no!" he cried. "I'll be trampled to death."

He began running, but he could hear the clovers getting closer and closer and —

The Brain bolted up in bed. Thank goodness it had only been a dream. But

wait — he was wet. But how could that be? The rain had been only in his dream.

Suddenly, a drop of water hit him on the forehead.

The Brain looked up. "Huh?"

Then another drop hit him. And a third. The Brain frowned and climbed out of bed to look out the window. It was raining.

"The water must be leaking in through the roof," he realized. "No wonder I got wet. That's not bad luck. These things just happen."

A little later the Brain settled himself on the floor. He had placed a bucket on his bed to catch the falling drops.

"It's not bad luck," he muttered to himself. "The roof must have had a leak already. Anyway, I'm sure the storm will let up soon."

But the storm didn't let up, at least not for a while. The drops came down faster.

The Brain groaned and pulled the blanket up over his head. After a while he fell back to sleep, hoping that by now the herd of four-leaf clovers was gone.

Chapter 6

• • • • • • • • • • •

When morning came, the Brain heard his mother's voice.

"Alan, you'd better wake up."

The Brain's eyes were still shut. "Is it an earthquake?" he asked sleepily.

"No," his mother went on, "I'm shaking your shoulder. It's eight-thirty, Alan."

The Brain's eyes popped open. "Eight-thirty! Oh, no! I'm late!"

His mother looked around. "Goodness, what happened here?"

The Brain jumped up. "You know, the usual. The roof . . . water . . . wild four-leaf clovers."

"Oh, really?" said his mother. "That must have been quite a dream."

A short while later, with toast hanging from his mouth, he rushed into the garage and took out his bike.

"Alan!" his mother called out to him through the kitchen window. "You forgot your lunch and your math homework."

The Brain ran back inside to get them. "Aha!" he said to himself. "If I was really having bad luck, I would have left them behind."

But at that moment, his father started backing the car out of the garage. And the Brain had gone back inside in such a hurry, he had left his bike lying right in the middle of the driveway.

His father didn't see it — until it was too late.

CRRRRRUNCH!

The Brain's bike was crushed, and his father's car had gotten a flat tire.

When the Brain came back outside, his father was standing there shaking his head.

"I don't believe this," said the Brain.

"The important thing," said his father, "is that no one was hurt. But how will you get to school?"

"Don't worry," said the Brain. "I'll be okay. Running will be good for my cardio-vascular system."

He ran along the sidewalk, hopping over the puddles as much as possible. But there had been a lot of rain, and it was hard to avoid them all.

Suddenly, he tripped — falling face first into a puddle of mud.

He got to his knees, dripping with mud, and looked around, thankful that his home-work and lunch had been thrown clear.

However, a dog was looking at them both.

"Hello. Nice doggie. Hungry doggie. No, no, not the homework. It's boring. So many numbers to digest. You can take my lunch!"

But the dog wasn't listening. It picked up the Brain's math homework, swallowed it in one gulp, and trotted off.

The Brain shook his head. This couldn't be happening! He looked around, half expecting to see a herd of four-leaf clovers.

Instead, a crow flew down and grabbed his lunch.

When the Brain finally got to school, he was a muddy mess. As he entered the class, Mr. Ratburn glanced at his watch.

"Nice of you to join us, Alan. Please leave your math homework on the desk."

"I don't have it." He paused. "A dog ate my homework."

Mr. Ratburn's mouth dropped open.

The Brain, though, was past caring. He

just shuffled to his desk and slumped into his chair.

Francine patted him on the arm. "Cheer up, Brain! Only six years and three hundred sixty-four days of bad luck to go."

Chapter 7

• • • • • • • • • • •

The Brain sat on Buster's bed, looking very upset.

"I can't take it anymore," he said.

Buster nodded. "Tell me what's happened."

The Brain laughed. "It might be quicker to say what hasn't happened. But anyway, let's see . . . a little storm cloud followed me around."

"Followed you?" said Buster.

The Brain nodded. "Raining on me all day. And then there was this dog. I guess you could say he kind of attached himself to my leg."

"Ouch!" said Buster.

"And let's not forget the Frisbee that hit me in the back of the head."

Buster looked impressed. "It sounds like you're lucky to be alive."

"I guess so. But that's not the worst thing. Friday the thirteenth is just two days away. Can you imagine what will happen then?" The Brain shuddered.

"It does sound pretty bad," Buster admitted.

"And so I've come to you," the Brain went on, "because you have nonscientific stuff down to a . . . well . . . science."

Buster held up a hand. "Say no more, Brain. You've come to the right place. I'm sure I can help. The way I see it, we just have to undo your bad luck with good luck."

The Brain laughed. "Oh, is that all?"

"Of course," Buster continued, "you can't do that at the snap of your fingers. You'll need to be prepared."

He opened his desk drawer and pulled out a box filled with little packets.

"You'll want salt, naturally," he said. "Whenever something bad happens, break a packet open and toss the salt over your left shoulder."

"My left shoulder?" The Brain frowned. "Why the left? Why not my right shoulder? What possible difference could the shoulder make?"

Buster shrugged. "It wasn't my idea. I'm just telling you the way it's done. But we're not finished yet."

He opened up his closet. Several dozen horseshoes were hanging on the inside of the door and piled in boxes.

"Wow!" said the Brain. "If you ever decide to become a blacksmith, you'll be all set."

Buster looked over his collection. "It's taken me years to get to this stage. Let's

see . . . I think a couple of Clydesdales should do the trick."

He took down two of the larger horseshoes and put them on the floor.

"Then you'll need some four-leaf clovers."

Buster took them out of a bureau drawer and put them and the horseshoes inside a black gym bag.

"And last but not least, my lucky hat." He reached up to the closet shelf and removed a bright purple jester's hat.

"What's so lucky about it?" asked the Brain.

"Once, when I was wearing this hat, everyone I knew gave me a present."

"Buster, that happened on your birthday!"

"Exactly! What a way to celebrate. You can't get any luckier than that."

He placed the hat on the Brain's head.

"Now you're all set!"

Chapter 8

• • • • • • • • • • • •

It took the Brain a very long time to get home because he was being so careful. He was wearing Buster's lucky hat and carrying his lucky charms, but was that really enough?

The Brain didn't want to take any chances. He carefully stepped over every crack in the sidewalk and threw salt over his left shoulder at each stop sign he passed.

And he kept a sharp lookout for black cats.

"So far, so good," he said as his house came within sight. Buster's lucky hat flopped on his head almost as if it were nodding in agreement.

As the Brain reached the front door, he straightened up. He'd made it! Home, sweet home. He felt like a great weight had been lifted from his shoulders.

"Whew!" he sighed.

The Brain wasn't sure if there was any special thing he should do before entering, but he wiped his feet very well. He figured it couldn't hurt.

"Hello!" he called out as he opened the door. "I'm home. Safely."

"That's nice, dear."

"Mom, what happened? Are you all right?"

The Brain's mother was stretched out on the floor with a washcloth across her forehead.

His mother smiled weakly. "Well, I've been better," she admitted. "But I've been worse, too." She patted the black gym bag

at her side. "I pulled a muscle in my back doing my exercises. Nice hat, dear."

"Oh, yeah, right." The Brain put down his bag next to his mother's. "It's a long story. Can I get you anything?"

"Actually, I'm all right for now."

"Really?"

"Really. I promise. Honest. No kidding."

"Okay," said the Brain. "I just wanted to make sure. Well, call if you need anything."

He went up to his room and closed the door behind him.

"I can't believe it!" he muttered.

He yanked off Buster's lucky hat and threw it on the bed.

"I go to the trouble of getting all this protection — and what happens? Does it help? No. The bad luck just bounces off me and hits my mother. What am I supposed to do about that? I'm a menace, that's what I am."

44

He looked out the window. Dark clouds were gathering overhead, and they seemed to be heading for his house. Meteorologically, he knew that wasn't possible. Weather didn't work that way, and clouds didn't have a mind of their own. They didn't have little meetings where they decided where they were going next.

Or did they?

"I used to think science had all the answers. And maybe it still does. But I don't even know the right questions anymore."

The Brain shook his fist at the clouds. "I know you're out there, Bad Luck, just waiting for another chance to pounce. Well, I'm not playing into your hands. I'm not leaving the house tomorrow! In fact, I may not ever leave it again."

Chapter 9

• • • • • • • • • • •

It was another beautiful day for a softball game. The sun was shining again. The sky was clear again.

And the game itself felt much the same, too. Mighty Mountain was crushing the Lakewood team. It was the bottom of the sixth inning, and Mighty Mountain was leading 7–2.

George was at the plate. He swung and missed.

"Steeerike three!" called the umpire. "Two outs."

"We're getting creamed!" muttered Francine from the bench. "Where *is* he?"

"He must be sick," said Arthur. "He wasn't in school today. It would make sense, with all the bad luck he's been having."

"He'd better be sick," muttered Francine. "Or he will be when I get done with him." She turned to Muffy. "Can I borrow your phone?"

Inside the Brain's house, the Brain was lying on the couch reading a book. When the phone rang, he picked it up.

"Hello?"

He listened for a moment, and then moved the receiver away from his ear. "Yes, Francine . . . oh, really? What's the score? Ah, well, I'm sorry to hear that. . . . What do you mean, *Sorry isn't enough?* Francine, do you know what day it is? It's Friday the thirteenth. And considering the way my luck has been going, I just can't risk it. Good-bye."

He hung up the phone and opened his book again.

Back at the game, it was now the bottom of the ninth. The score was 9–6. But the Lakewood team was threatening to score with one out and the bases loaded. Francine was on first, Arthur was on second, and Binky was on third.

"Come on, Muffy," they called out. "You can do it. Just make contact."

The next pitch came in. Muffy swung at it — and missed.

"Steeerike three!"

Arthur sighed. "Maybe we should just give up. The game's almost over, anyway."

"Hey, guys!" Buster shouted from the bench. "Look!"

The Brain had arrived, clutching a black gym bag to his chest.

Francine was surprised. "I thought you didn't want to risk it," she called out.

The Brain put down the bag. "I realized that no matter where I am, I'll have bad luck with me. So I thought it would be nice at least to have company."

"Your timing is good," said Buster. "It's your spot in the order."

The Brain took the bat from Muffy and walked up to the plate. He spit on the handle and grabbed it with both hands. Then he stepped in.

The pitcher wound up — and released the pitch.

The Brain waited, waited, waited — and then . . .

WHACK!

The Brain started for first base, then he hesitated, looking at the black gym bag by the bench. Was it staring at him? Was it safe to continue? Well, he hadn't tripped yet. So he kept going.

As he rounded first base, the ball looked like it was going to hit a lamppost. The

Brain waved at the ball wildly, hoping it would stay clear.

And it did! It even missed the tree and went over the back fence.

The Brain had hit a home run.

"Lakewood wins, ten to nine!" shouted the umpire as the Brain crossed home plate. "Game over!"

The whole team came forward and surrounded him.

"You did it!"

"What a shot!"

"Way to go, Brain!"

Chapter 10

• • • • • • • • • • • •

A little later, Arthur, Buster, Francine, and the Brain were walking away from the diamond.

"So what brought you back?" asked Francine.

"I did some figuring," said the Brain. "Assuming an average life expectancy, there will be another one hundred and fifty Friday-the-thirteenths in my lifetime. It did not seem practical to spend them all hiding at home."

"Well," said Arthur, "now I know how to break seven years of bad luck. I just have to hit a grand slam."

"Hey," said Buster. "Can I have my charms back? You probably won't need them for a while."

"Sure," said the Brain. He handed Buster the gym bag.

Buster opened it. "Hey! Where's my stuff? What did you do with my lucky hat? And what am I supposed to do with this?"

He pulled out a pink headband.

The Brain frowned. "Wait! Those are my mom's clothes. I must have taken the wrong bag . . ." He paused. "Do you know what this means? I've proved my hypothesis! Superstitions really *are* false!"

"Hold on there," said Buster. "You haven't proven that at all. What you've proven is that these are very lucky gym clothes."

Arthur and Francine stepped up for a closer look.

"Could I borrow these lucky socks?" asked Arthur.

"And I'll try the sweatband," said Francine.

They started to walk away as they continued to look through the bag.

The Brain looked at his friends and shook his head. "Well, if you can't beat 'em, join 'em!"

And he ran to catch up, jumping over every crack in the sidewalk.